IF I HAD A ROBOT

dan yaccarino

viking

VIKING   Published by the Penguin Group
Penguin Books USA Inc., 375 Hudson Street, New York, New York 10014, U.S.A.
Penguin Books Ltd, 27 Wrights Lane, London W8 5TZ, England
Penguin Books Australia Ltd, Ringwood, Victoria, Australia
Penguin Books Canada Ltd, 10 Alcorn Avenue, Toronto, Ontario, Canada M4V 3B2
Penguin Books (N.Z.) Ltd, 182-190 Wairau Road, Auckland 10, New Zealand
Penguin Books Ltd, Registered Offices: Harmondsworth, Middlesex, England
First published in 1996 by Viking, a division of Penguin Books USA Inc.
1   3   5   7   9   10   8   6   4   2
Copyright © Dan Yaccarino, 1996   All rights reserved
LIBRARY OF CONGRESS CATALOGING-IN-PUBLICATION DATA
Yaccarino, Dan.   If I had a robot / by Dan Yaccarino.   p.   cm.
Summary : Phil imagines the advantages of having a robot,
from feeding it his vegetables to becoming king of the playground.
ISBN 0-670-86936-8   [1. Robots—Fiction. 2. Behavior—Fiction.]   I. Title.
PZ7.Y125If 1996 [E]—dc20   95-26444 CIP AC
Printed in Singapore   Set in Humanist

SPECIAL THANKS TO THE ROBOT FROM "LOST IN SPACE," TOBOR, ROBBIE THE ROBOT, GIGANTOR, THE ROCK 'EM SOCK 'EM ROBOTS AND EVERY SPECIAL MECHANICAL PAL NOT MENTIONED HERE.

"Phil," Mom said, "you can't leave the dinner table until you finish your vegetables."

Boy!
I hate
vegetables!
I wish
someone
else would
eat them
for me!

I bet if I had a robot he would eat those vegetables at my command!

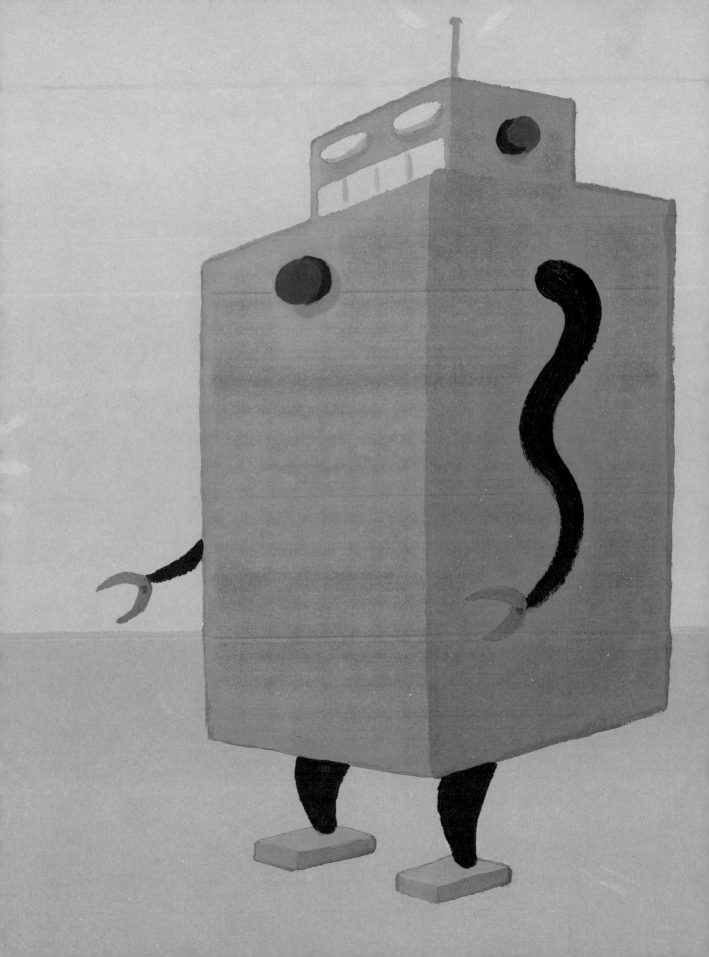

Yessiree!
With just
the flick
of a switch,
he'd eat
all my
lima
beans,
cauli-
flower,
and
brussels
sprouts.
Yuck!

I could get him to
take my bath.

And piano lessons, too!

Boy! He could do everything

I don't want to do!

Why, he could even kiss my Aunt Louise!

And
go to
school
so I
don't
have
to!

No hotshot could ever
hit a home run when
we're in left field.

And those kids wouldn't dare pick on me if I had a robot. Gee, I'd be king of the play-ground!

Hey! With my robot
I could be king
of the whole world!

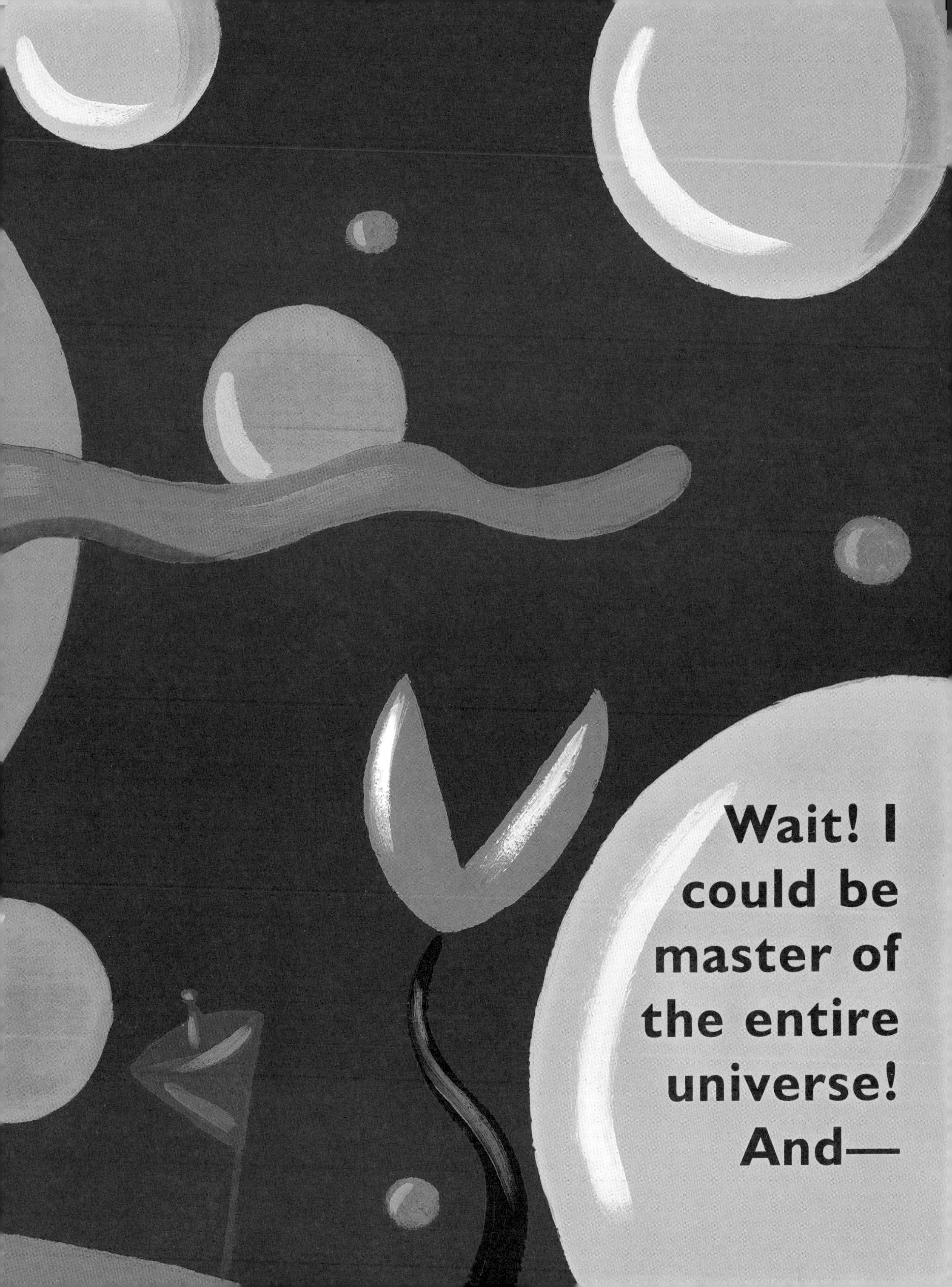

Wait! I could be master of the entire universe! And—

"Oh Phil . . ." my mom called. "Whoever eats their vegetables gets chocolate cake for dessert!"

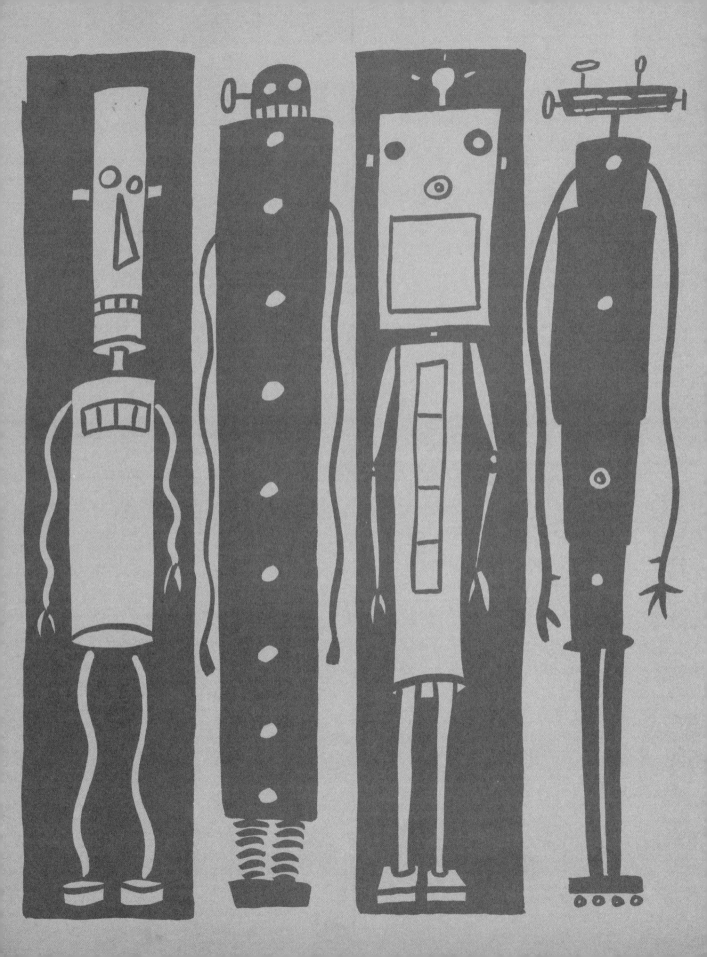